"Salem called the Psychic Pals Hotline?"

"That's the one we saw on TV!" Sabrina remembered. "Salem! I can't believe you called them. I thought you said they were ridiculous."

"I did. They are. And now I am," Salem mumbled. He felt totally humiliated.

"You know you're going to have to pay for this call," Aunt Zelda declared.

Pay for it? How could he pay for the call? He had just lost all his money in the stock market—thanks to that phony psychic's advice!

"Uh, can you bill me?" Salem asked nervously. "I'm a little short of cash right now."

"No cash?" Zelda asked. "No problem. We'll just let you *work* it off."

Sabrina, the Teenage Witch™
Salem's Tails™

Available from MINSTREL Books

Sabrina The Teenage Witch™

Salem's Tails™

PSYCHIC KITTY

Cathy East Dubowski

Based on Characters Appearing in Archie Comics

And based upon the television series
Sabrina, The Teenage Witch
Created for television by Nell Scovell
Developed for television by Jonathan Schmock

Illustrated by Mark Dubowski

A
MINSTREL®
BOOK

Published by POCKET BOOKS
New York   London   Toronto   Sydney   Tokyo   Singapore

A MINSTREL PAPERBACK *Original*

A Minstrel Book published by
POCKET BOOKS, a division of Simon & Schuster Inc.
1230 Avenue of the Americas, New York, NY 10020

Sabrina, The Teenage Witch: Salem's Tails
Based on characters appearing in Archie Comics
And the television series created by Nell Scovell
Developed for television by Jonathan Schmock

Salem quotes taken from the following episodes:
"Suspicious Minds" written by Dan Berendsen
"The Big Sleep" written by Sheldon Bull

ISBN: 0-671-02382-9

First Minstrel Books printing May 1999

10 9 8 7 6 5 4 3 2 1

A MINSTREL BOOK and colophon are registered trademarks of Simon & Schuster Inc.

SABRINA THE TEENAGE WITCH and all related titles, logos and characters are trademarks of Archie Comics Publications, Inc.

Cover photo by Pat Hill Studio

Printed in the U.S.A.

To Elizabeth Shiflett—

Who seems almost psychic in her abilities to take care of authors. Thanks, Liz, for everything you do!

—CED

You know, nothing says "I'm grateful" more than cash.

—*Salem*

Chapter 1

"*Scat, cat!*"

Salem the cat barely heard the words. He was curled up on the couch in the Spellman sisters' Victorian house. It had taken him a good twenty minutes to get his position just right for a *purrr*fect catnap.

No way I'm moving for at least six months, he thought, half asleep.

"Excuse me . . . Salem . . . ?"

"Zzzzzzz . . . I'm sorry," Salem mumbled, as if talking in his sleep. "I cannot

take your call at this time. Please hang up and try again later. Much, much later."

There. That should do it. He wiggled deeper into the couch cushions and sighed.

Suddenly Salem felt himself flying straight up into the air.

"Meowrrr!" he shrieked.

He was going to hit the ceiling!

He closed his eyes. He hated to see a cat get hurt. Especially when he was the endangered cat.

But he didn't hit the ceiling. Instead he floated in the air like a cat-shaped cloud.

When his pounding heart slowed a little, he peeled open one eye.

Sabrina Spellman and her aunt Hilda sat down on the couch. *Hey, right in the warm spot where I was sleeping,* Salem thought.

"Just because you two are witches doesn't mean you have the right to push poor little defenseless kitties like me around," Salem complained.

Sabrina and Hilda were used to Salem's whining.

"We weren't pushing you around," Sabrina pointed out. "We were just moving you over."

Aunt Hilda shrugged. "The couch is for witches and humans. You cats can sleep anywhere."

"That is *not* true," Salem said. "Besides, you didn't move me over. You moved me up."

"Whatever." Sabrina slipped off her sneakers and curled up on the couch.

Right in my spot, Salem pouted.

"Uh, hello down there!" Salem called from the ceiling. "I hate to be a pest. But, well—*COULD YOU GET ME DOWN FROM HERE?*"

"Oops! Sorry." Sabrina wiggled her finger and—

3

Plop! Salem landed softly on the arm of the couch.

"Thanks," Salem muttered. He groomed his ruffled fur with his tongue. "I ought to report them to the ASPCA," he grumbled.

"I heard that," Aunt Hilda said.

Salem kneaded the upholstered arm of the couch with his paws, trying to get it just right. "So, tell me. What's so important that you just have to sit on the couch to do it?"

Sabrina picked up the remote control and clicked on the TV. "Aunt Hilda and I want to watch an old movie."

Salem rolled his eyes as the opening credits appeared on the TV screen. "I gave up my best nap all week for a movie that's not even in color?"

Sabrina and Hilda snuggled down into the couch.

"Popcorn?" Hilda asked.

"I'd love some," Sabrina replied.

Hilda zapped the coffee table. A huge bowl appeared. It overflowed with popcorn.

But not just regular popcorn. Sparkly Witchy-Pop Popcorn. Popcorn enchanted by a magic spell.

"Cinnamon sugar!" Hilda said.

Cinnamon-colored sparkles shimmered up from the bowl.

Hilda scooped up a handful. "Mmm. Delicious! What do you think, Sabrina?"

Sabrina tasted the popcorn. "It's good. But, well, I'm kind of in the mood for something different."

Hilda grinned. "Be my guest."

"So, all I have to do is call out a different flavor, right?" Sabrina asked.

Hilda nodded. "And the magic spell automatically changes the popcorn."

Sabrina thought. "Okay, how about . . . chocolate chip!"

Chocolately sparkles snowed down over the bowl.

"Oooh, excellent idea!" Hilda told her niece.

Sabrina and Hilda reached for another handful. They popped the popcorn into their mouths. Just as . . .

"Anchovy and liver!" Salem crowed.

"Ewww!"

Sabrina and Aunt Hilda spit out their popcorn. With a swish of his tail, Salem buried his face in the bowl.

"Salem Saberhagen!" Sabrina shrieked, holding her nose. "Warn us before you do something like that, okay?"

"Hey, I have to grab for the magic whenever I can," Salem explained.

Salem hadn't always been a sleek black American shorthair cat. He'd once been a powerful warlock—a male witch. He had been able to do magic. But then he got into hot water when he tried to take over the world. A big no-no. To punish him, the Witches' Council had turned him into a cat for a hundred years.

He'd lost all his powers—except one.

He could still talk. Usually he used that power to complain.

"Oh, no, not another commercial," Salem groaned. "The movie just started."

"That's what I hate about human TV," Aunt Hilda muttered. "You can't fast-forward the commercials."

"Oh, get this one," Sabrina said.

A man with a white beard gazed at them over a crystal ball. "Friends, are you sad? Lonesome? Worried about the future? Do you have a difficult choice to make? Do you wish someone could help you decide what to do?"

"Yes!" Salem shouted. "How about: Should I change the channel?"

"Worry no more, friends," the psychic

7

continued. "I want to be your pal. Your Psychic Pal."

"Oh, brother," Hilda said.

Then the camera switched to a woman who was wearing too much blue eye shadow. "Hi. My name is Shirley," she said in a twangy accent. "A month ago I was so depressed. I was broke. My husband left me. And I had a wart on my nose that wouldn't go away."

Sabrina hooted with laughter.

"What a loser," Salem muttered.

"Then I called the Psychic Pals Hotline," Shirley went on. "I asked them what to do."

The camera panned back to show a huge mansion behind her. A shiny new sports car was parked in the drive.

"Now look at me," Shirley said. "I am rich. I have a handsome new boyfriend."

A good-looking guy in a blue blazer

walked on-screen and wrapped Shirley in a mink coat, then gave her a big hug.

"Even the wart on my nose is almost gone!" She smiled at the camera. "Thanks, Psychic Pals Hotline!"

Then the bearded psychic came back on. "So, friends, why wait? You, too, can have all your dreams come true. Call the Psychic Pals Hotline today!"

The phone number flashed on the screen in big black letters. A lot of tiny type ran quickly across the bottom of the screen, but Salem couldn't read what it said.

"I can't believe anybody falls for this garbage," Aunt Hilda said. "It's so totally fake."

"Yeah," Salem agreed. "Ridiculous."

The movie came back on.

Salem stood up and arched his back, pretending to stretch. "Ah, me. I think I'm going to call it a night," he said with a yawn.

Sabrina looked at the clock. "Salem, what gives? It's only eight-fifteen."

Salem shrugged. "I guess laughing at the infomercials wore me out."

Salem leaped from the couch and slowly padded up the stairs. But when he got near the top—where no one could see him—he bolted toward Sabrina's room.

Once inside, he stood up on his hind legs and pawed at the door to close it.

It wasn't to block out the noise of the TV.

It wasn't so he could rest in peace.

It was so no one could hear what he was up to.

Salem listened at the door to make sure no one was coming. Then he leaped onto Sabrina's bed.

Salem needed to make a phone call. A *secret* phone call.

Lucky for Salem, Sabrina had a phone with a speakerphone. He could poke the numbers with his paw. Then he could talk and listen on the speakerphone. He didn't even have to hold the receiver.

Which was good. It was very hard to hold things without fingers.

Salem tapped in a phone number. The phone rang and rang. At last someone answered.

"Hello," Salem whispered into the phone. "This is Salem S. I need some advice."

He glanced around. The door was still closed.

"Tell me," he asked, "should I buy or sell my stocks?"

Salem hadn't called his stockbroker. He hadn't called a financial planner.

Salem was looking for a different kind of advice.

Salem had called the Psychic Pals Network!

Chapter 2

P lop!

Two days later Salem rushed to the front door. He pawed at the wood. "Hel-lo!" he called out. "I could use a hand here—literally."

Salem could push a door closed. But with paws, it was impossible to open one.

"Gotta go—out?" Sabrina teased as she came down the stairs.

"No," Salem snapped. "My copy of the

Wall Street Journal just hit the front porch. Quick! Open the door!"

Sabrina opened the door, and Salem dashed outside. Frantically he clawed at the yellow plastic bag that held the morning paper.

Sabrina rolled her eyes. "Are you going to *read* it? Or shred it into kitty litter?"

"Are you going to make fun of me or help me?" Salem shot back.

"Here, let me do that." Sabrina picked up the newspaper and carried it to the kitchen. She helped Salem spread it open on the breakfast table. Then she opened it to Salem's favorite page—the stock report. It told how much each stock was worth.

"Happy reading," she said, shaking her head. Then she zapped herself up a tall stack of whole-wheat blueberry waffles. Plus a copy of *YW* (as in *Young and Witchy*) magazine.

Salem's whiskers trembled as he ran

down the list of stocks. How much money had he made?

Two nights ago he had talked to a very, very friendly Psychic Pal. He had advised Salem to buy a certain stock. He had predicted it would make Salem millions!

Gosh, those Psychic Pals really care! Salem had thought at the time. He was on the phone with his stockbroker for only a few minutes, but his personal Psychic Pal had talked to him for *hours!*

Now he was eager to see just how *rich, rich, rich* he had become!

Where is it, where is it? he thought impatiently.

There! He found the name of his stock. He read across the line to read the numbers.

What!

Salem's eyes bulged open. He made a nasty choking sound.

Sabrina glanced up from her magazine and waffles. "Ewww. Another hair ball?"

Salem could barely gasp out an answer. "No . . . just a little . . . *gagh!* . . . frog . . . in my throat. . . ."

Sabrina reached out to pet her kitty. "Salem, are you all right?"

"Could you . . . get me a bowl of . . . water, please?"

Sabrina went to the sink and turned on the tap.

Meanwhile, Salem rubbed his eyes with his little black paw. He took a deep breath.

Then he looked at the newspaper again.

It couldn't be true.

But it was!

Psychic Pal? HAH! Salem thought. *How about Psycho Rip-off Artist!*

Salem nearly wept.

All his stock had gone down in price. Way, way down. That meant Salem's stock was nearly worthless. He was broke!

"I'm ru-u-uined!" he moaned. "What a scam. What total *fakes!*"

Sabrina set a bowl of water down in front of him. "What did you say, Salem?"

"Uh . . . *flakes!*" Salem choked out. "I said *flakes*. How about a bowl of some delicious, nutritious corn*flakes* for breakfast?"

Aunt Zelda came into the kitchen just in time to hear that. "Why, Salem, I'm so pleased to see you eating a sensible breakfast for a change. I'll fix it for you."

She zapped a small bowl of kitty cornflakes next to his water bowl.

"Sensible. Yeah. Right." Salem buried his furry little head in his paws. *Stupid is more like it! I'm ruined!* he sobbed to himself. *What a fool I was!*

He glanced at Sabrina and Zelda. They were staring at him curiously.

But he couldn't tell them what happened. He was too ashamed. He had taken the advice of a fake psychic. And he'd lost all his money!

Salem leaped to the floor.

"Salem—where are you going?" Aunt Zelda asked. "What about your corn-flakes? They'll get soggy."

"Uh, I'm not hungry all of a sudden," Salem said. "Just toss them."

"Throw out good food?" Aunt Zelda exclaimed. "When there are—"

"Starving kitties in New Delhi, I know," Salem muttered.

Aunt Zelda snapped her fingers, and the cereal bowl disappeared. "They'll be waiting for you—tomorrow morning."

"I hate leftovers," Salem muttered. But at least he was free to run upstairs. There, alone in Sabrina's room, he could grieve over his lost wealth.

Lucky for me it's my little secret, he thought. *No one will ever know.*

17

Chapter 3

ne week later Zelda came in the front door with the mail—and screamed!

She had just opened an envelope.

Sabrina ran to her side in the front entry hall. "Aunt Zelda! What's wrong? Are you all right?"

Her aunt's eyes glowed as if they were on fire. "Salem!" she shouted. Thunder and lightning rumbled and flashed through the house.

Salem was in the living room—napping

on the couch again. *I think I had better relocate,* he thought nervously. He tried to sneak upstairs.

But Zelda was quicker. With a flick of her wrist—*Zing! Poof!*—she made the stairs disappear.

"Hey, no fair!" Salem meowed.

Hilda popped in just then from a trip to the Other Realm Outlet Mall. "What's going on?" she asked as she magically zapped all her packages to her room. She glanced down at the cowering black cat. "Oh, no. Is Salem in the doghouse again?"

Aunt Zelda ran her hand through her shoulder-length blond hair and nodded. "Just wait till you see what he did *this* time."

She held her mail where Salem could see. "Do you know what this is, buster?"

Salem glanced at the paper. "Looks like a bill."

"What kind of bill?" Aunt Zelda asked.

1 9

Salem looked closer.

Gulp!

"Ph-ph-phone bill?" he stuttered.

Aunt Zelda tapped the paper with a manicured nail. "Read this line."

Salem read.

It was his phone call to the Psychic Pals Hotline. He'd forgotten about that one little detail. All those nine hundred numbers worked by billing your call to your phone number.

"Uh-oh . . ."

Salem had thought a call to the Psychic Pals Hotline was $3.99.

It was. But not for the whole call.

It was $3.99 a minute! *No wonder my "pal" wanted to talk for hours! The more he talked, the more money he earned from suckers like . . . me.*

Zelda shook her head. "Once I saw the charges, I knew Sabrina wasn't responsible. How could you fall for such a scam,

Salem Saberhagen? These TV psychics are such total fakes!"

Aunt Hilda took the bill and read. "Oh, no. You're kidding me. Salem called the Psychic Pals Hotline?"

"That's the one we saw on TV!" Sabrina remembered. "Salem! I can't believe you called them. I thought you said they were ridiculous."

"I did. They are. And now I am," Salem mumbled. He felt totally humiliated.

But that wasn't the worst of it.

"You know you're going to have to pay for this call," Aunt Zelda declared.

Pay for it? How could he pay for the call? He had just lost all his money in the stock market—thanks to that phony psychic's advice!

"Uh, can you bill me?" Salem asked nervously. "I'm a little short of cash right now."

"No cash?" Zelda asked. "No problem."

"Really?" Salem asked. Zelda sounded like one of those used-car salesmen on TV. "What do you mean?"

Hilda and Zelda shared a knowing look.

Aunt Zelda smiled. "We'll just let you work it off . . ."

". . . by doing chores!" Aunt Hilda finished.

"Work?" Salem gagged. "Ch-Chores?"

Soon Salem was down on his paws—scrubbing the kitchen floor with *w-w-w-water!*

This is disgusting! Salem thought. He slipped his paw under the strap on the back of the scrub brush. He dipped the scrub brush into the soapy water. Then he scrubbed the brush around in circles on the filthy floor.

This is just plain mean, Salem thought miserably. *They're witches. All they have to do is point and the whole house is clean. But noooooo, they have to make me do it—'the old-fashioned way.' With my bare paws!*

"This is an outrage!" Salem muttered. "Cat labor! It's got to be against the law!"

I've got to think of some way to make some money—fast—so I can pay those meanies back, he thought. *But how?*

Chapter 4

$\mathcal{G}$ood afternoon, friend! You've reached Salem's Psychic Hotline—'Advice from the Other Realm.' If you've got the dime, we've got the time. How may we cheat—er, help you?"

Salem struggled to keep from snickering as he straightened his purple star-spangled cape. He shoved his red, jeweled turban up out of his eyes. He knew the person on the other end couldn't see his costume. But it helped him to get in the proper mood.

Salem had come up with the perfect get-rich scheme: He'd started his own psychic hotline!

After all, he thought, *I'm way ahead of those other guys. I've got smarts. Real financial experience. And enough charisma to charm the socks off Socks.*

I should be able to fool any fool foolish enough to call, he had decided. Mortals were so easy to con anyway.

And it was perfect. None of the callers would ever suspect they were talking to a cat!

"Hello," said his first customer, a woman. "My name is Christel Ea—"

"No last names," Salem interrupted.

"Okay. Well, I'm trying to decide about getting a pet," she said.

"A pet." *Smart move*, he thought.

"But I've never had a pet before," she went on. "Should I get one? Where should I get one? How much should I spend?

And should I get a cat? How about a great big dog?"

Salem turned away from the phone so he could gag. "As if there's a choice," he muttered.

Then he went back on the line. "Psychic Salem hears your question. I pause now to gaze into the future. . . . *Ummm* . . . *oooh* . . . *meowwwl* . . ." He moaned and groaned, to make it sound as if he were going into a psychic trance.

"Are you all right?" Christel asked in a worried voice.

"I'm fine," Salem snapped, a little insulted that his fine acting was so unappreciated. "I'm *trying* to make a psychic connection."

"Oh. I thought you were sick or something."

Salem rolled his eyes. *I guess when you have a job dealing with the public, you have to put up with all kinds.*

But he had to stretch the phone call out a little. The longer he kept the person on the phone, the more money he made, right? *"Ummmmm, purrrrrr, yeowwwl . . ."*

"Well?" Christel said impatiently. "I can't stay on all day."

"Hey, you can't rush psychic channeling," Salem replied. "The images are still cloudy. . . ." But he figured he had better cut to the chase, so she wouldn't hang up. "Oh, wait—yes. Yes! It's becoming clearer now. I can see . . ."

"What?" Christel asked breathlessly.

"I can see an animal. A loving animal. It's . . . it's—"

"What? What!"

"I see it now!" Salem exclaimed, gazing at himself in Sabrina's full-length mirror. "It's a cat!"

"A cat?"

"Yes!" Salem replied. He preened, admiring his sleek black coat in the reflected

image. "A black American shorthair—and darn proud of it!"

Hey, he thought. *Why not recommend the best?*

"Are you sure?" the woman asked. "I was sort of thinking about a dog. Something little and fluffy maybe."

"Ewww," Salem said.

"What?"

"I—I mean, *you* . . . should definitely get a cat. Cross my paws—er, fingers—and hope to spit."

"Are you sure?" Christel asked.

"Salem says what Salem sees. . . . The psychic vibes are clear. This cat will bring great love, harmony, and happiness to your home."

"I'll do it!" Christel said. "And thank you, Salem. You've been so helpful."

"Tell all your friends about me!" Salem told her.

"I will! Goodbye!" Then the woman hung up.

"Woo-hoo!" Salem cried—borrowing one of Sabrina's favorite expressions. He pumped the air with his paw. "Is this easy or what?"

He smiled dreamily. Just imagine all the wonderful money he would earn. He could rebuild his stock portfolio. He could buy that new cat toy he'd admired in the pet store window. He could order smoked salmon delivered direct to his door! He could . . .

The phone rang again.

"Hello! You've reached Salem's Psychic Hotline—'Advice from the Other Realm.' If you've got a buck, I'll bring you good luck. How may I help you?"

Someone mumbled something in a deep croaky voice.

Salem couldn't understand a word. "Excuse me. Could you speak up, please?"

The caller hung up. The dial tone buzzed in Salem's ears.

"Darn!" Salem complained. "I've got to do better than that!" He couldn't make money on short calls.

The phone rang again. Salem's paw shot toward the speakerphone button—

"Sa-lem!"

Uh-oh! Zelda! She was home from her International Scientists Potluck Luncheon.

Salem yanked off his cape and turban and dragged them under Sabrina's bed. Lucky for him the phone had stopped ringing!

Then he crouched among the dust bunnies and peeked out under the bed ruffle.

"Salem? Are you in here?" Zelda poked her head in the doorway holding a . . .

Good grief, it couldn't be!

Ewww! A toilet bowl brush!

That did it. He had to earn lots of cash—fast! Or they'd have him scrubbing . . .

30

No. I won't even think it!

He held his breath till Zelda closed the door and went away.

Salem poked his nose out from under the bed ruffle.

His scam was so fabulous. He could really rake in a fortune.

But he would have to be careful. It was going to be tricky running a psychic hotline from the home of three witches—especially with Zelda and Hilda chasing him down for chores!

Chapter 5

That night Salem lucked out.

Hilda had been summoned before an emergency meeting of the Witches' Council to explain a parking ticket she got on Mars. Zelda went along to help.

That left only Sabrina.

She stood in front of her full-length mirror and zapped her way through several outfits. At last she narrowed it down to two. "Jeans? Or a long skirt?" With a snap of her fingers, she flicked back and forth between the two outfits a few times.

Just pick one and go! Salem wanted to shout. He was eager to get to work.

Sabrina twirled a strand of blond hair around her fingertip, saying "I think I'll go with the skirt. I think. What do you think?"

"The skirt is divine!" he exclaimed. "It makes you look ten pounds thinner."

"Thanks a lot." She grabbed her purse from the bed and gave Salem's head a pat. "Gotta go. I'm meeting Harvey and Val at the Slicery to study for our history test."

"I believe you," Salem said. *Not!*

Sabrina just rolled her eyes and dashed for the door.

"Uh, when will you be home?" Salem asked.

Sabrina frowned. "Why do you need to know?"

"So . . . so I won't worry," Salem purred.

"Oh, Salem, that's sweet." She came back to give him a quick hug.

"Better hurry," he said, trying to hide his impatience.

Sabrina was halfway out the door when the phone rang. She started to turn back.

"I'll get it," Salem told her.

"But what if it's—"

"Just go!" Salem said. "It's probably a salesman. And I don't want you to miss a single minute of fun with your friends."

"Thanks, Salem," Sabrina said. "You're a real sweetheart."

"I know."

Sabrina tilted her head, then pointed at the bed. *Zap!* A pretty plate full of kitty snacks appeared right in front of Salem's drooling jaws.

"Wow!" Salem cried. "Sardines, popcorn shrimp, clams on the half shell . . ." Even the crackers were little tiny goldfish.

"Thanks, Sabrina." He slurped up a sardine and sighed.

Sabrina grinned. "See what can happen when you're nice to a teenage witch?" With a quick wave, she ran out the door.

Ring, ring.

Salem pawed the speakerphone button. "Um, hold one moment, please," he whispered, trying to sound like a secretary. He waited till he heard the front door slam behind Sabrina.

Whew! That was close!

"Good evening! You've reached Salem's Psychic Hotline—'Advice from the Other Realm.' If you've got the dough, I'll tell you all I know. How may I help you, my friend?"

"This is Mac Dou—"

"No last names, please!" Salem said. He held up a clamshell and let a clam slide into his mouth.

"I need some advice," Mac said. He sounded really upset.

"In what realm of your life?" Salem mumbled around a mouthful of seafood.

"Uh, I guess you'd say money and career."

"Whoa," Salem said. "Have *you* come to the right place!"

"Uh . . . I don't know. Have I?"

"You bet!" Salem exclaimed, swishing his tail. "Money and wealth are my favorite topics."

"Well, it's about my job, really," the caller said. "I work at a really big company. I have a very important job. But I have to work long hours. There's a lot of stress."

"So . . . what's your question?" Salem asked. He slipped his jeweled turban on to help him get in the psychic mood.

"Should I keep my job?" Mac asked.

"Or should I follow my heart and do something I've always wanted to do?"

"And what is that?" Salem asked.

"Work in a bookstore."

"Excuse me?"

"There's this job opening at my favorite bookstore," Mac explained. "It's just a clerk's job. But reading is my passion. I love being around books. I thought I might be happier at this job. What do you think, Salem? Should I quit my stressful job and follow my heart?"

Salem threw himself into his psychic act. He closed his eyes and made strange moaning sounds. *"Hmmm . . . yeowwwl . . . burp*—excuse me."* He shoved the tempting plate of snacks aside. "There are mists . . . I cannot see . . . Concentrate!" he told the caller.

"Can you see the future?" Mac asked desperately. "What should I do?"

Salem moaned, then said, "The answer

is unclear. I need more information." He thought a moment, then asked, "What is your salary at your current job?"

The man told him. It was a large salary. A *very* large salary. The number had lots and lots of zeros at the end.

Salem jumped in excitement. He was hyperventilating! *This nut wants to trade that in for a job at a bookstore?*

"Are you out of your mind?" he screeched into the phone. Then he cleared his throat. "I, uh, what I mean is, you must be out of your mind worrying which path to choose. Let me think . . ."

One and one-half seconds later Salem said, "Hang on to the money!"

"You mean keep my current job?" Mac asked.

"Yes!" Salem replied. "There are people living on cat food in this world . . ." *And I'm one of them,* he thought. "You don't know how lucky you are to have a job that pays so much money."

"Well," the man said. "They say money can't buy happiness. . . ."

"Forget 'they'!" Salem argued. "I get so tired of hearing 'they' say this. And 'they' say that. Forget 'they.' Listen to Salem. Hold on to that job—whatever you do. It is the smartest choice for a future of wealth and security."

"Well, okay. If you're sure," Mac said.

"I am sure." Salem purred. "And please, feel free to call whenever you want—any time, day or night. Salem will be glad to talk to you. For hours. And don't forget to tell all your friends about me."

"Thank you." Then the man hung up.

Salem popped a popcorn shrimp into his mouth and sighed in delight. *Whiskers! but I'm good!* he thought.

The phone rang again. Salem swallowed quickly, then jabbed the speakerphone

button. "You've reached Salem's Psychic Hotline. If you've got the dollar, Salem will holler. . . ."

Mumble, mumble.

Oh, no. It was that person with the deep croaky voice again.

"Speak up, please."

No answer.

"I can't help you if I can't hear you," Salem tried.

He waited, but all he could hear were strange burplike sounds.

"Hey, take my advice—and buy some cough drops! You've got a frog in your throat!" Salem said.

Hummm. The line went dead.

"Good riddance to bad customers," Salem muttered.

The phone kept ringing. Salem answered every call with flair and insight.

By the time Sabrina came home that night, Salem had answered dozens of calls.

I'm gonna be rich, he told himself as he curled up on the foot of her bed to go to sleep. But he realized there was even more to it than that.

I'm good, Salem admitted to himself. He had finally found his calling. He could get rich—and help his fellow man at the same time.

Hey, maybe this could even count toward those community service hours the Witches' Council is making me do.

He fell asleep, dreaming of how wonderful he was.

The next day Sabrina went to school as usual. Hilda and Zelda had another appointment with the Witches' Council.

Salem looked forward to another day of helping people—and getting paid to do it!

The phone rang. Salem snatched it up. He was really getting into this.

4 1

"Greetings! You've reached Salem's Psychic Hotline—"

"Psychic swindle is more like it!" a woman shouted.

Uh-oh. It was the woman who had called yesterday about getting a pet. "Uh, hello, Christel. How are you?"

"Terrible!" she exclaimed angrily.

"Tell me all about it," Salem purred. "Then I can advise you what to do."

"I got a cat—like you told me I should!" she shouted into the phone.

"It didn't work out?" Salem guessed.

"Hah!" Christel exclaimed. "If you're such a super psychic, how come you didn't foresee that my husband is *allergic* to cats!"

"Oops!" Salem said. "I, uh, guess I wasn't tuned in to his aura."

"Aura my foot!" Christel said. "You're a fake! You're a scam artist! Why, I ought to report you to—"

"Uh, sorry, I've got another call!" Salem hung up fast. His breath came out in a whoosh.

If Salem weren't a cat, he would have been blushing. *Oh, well,* he told himself. *You can't win them all. I bet no psychic gets it right a hundred percent of the time.*

The phone rang again.

"My hat! I need my hat to feel psychic!" He found his turban and slipped it on, then put on his purple star cape, too.

Then he answered the call. "Salem's Psychic Hotline! I see all, I—"

"Not!" a man shouted.

Uh-oh. It was Mac, the man who called yesterday about job advice.

"Hello, again," Salem said politely. "How are you?"

"If you're so psychic, how come you don't know?" the man snapped.

Good question, Salem thought. "Give me a hint."

"If you can see into the future, how come you couldn't see that my company was going to announce a merger today?" the man exclaimed. "And that I was going to be laid off from my job?"

Salem gasped. "You mean fired? From that lovely high-paying job?"

"You got it, buster!"

"Oh," Salem replied, scrambling for an excuse. "Well, sometimes the stars can interfere with—"

"Yeah, right."

"Well, fate does sometimes step in to alter our choices," Salem tried. "But look at the bright side!" *I'm a cat, right? I always land on my feet.* "Now I see true happiness in your future. For now you are free to take the job in the bookstore."

"No, I'm not!" Mac growled.

"Why not?" Salem asked.

"Because—they already gave the job to someone else!" he shouted back. "Now I don't have a job at all!"

Uh-oh. "Gotta go!" Salem gulped and hung up the phone.

Salem buried his head in his paws. He wasn't doing so hot here. If word got around that he gave out bad advice, no one would call his hotline. Then how would he ever make any money?

Maybe you should just be a little more vague with your advice, he told himself. *That's how those real fakers do it.*

Just like with fortune cookies and horoscopes, Salem told himself. *Say something so general it will seem to come true for anybody.*

The phone rang.

Salem bit his paw. Was it a fresh chump—er, customer? Or someone else from last night calling to complain about bad advice?

I wish I really were psychic, he thought nervously. *Then I would know whether or not to answer the phone!*

But being a cat, his curiosity got the best of him. Also his greed.

He pressed the speakerphone button. "Hello," he purred. "Salem's Psychic Hotline. If you've got the dime, I've got the time. . . ."

"Salem!"

Uh-oh.

Sabrina had just appeared in the middle of her room.

"I'm busted!" Salem moaned.

Chapter 6

"Salem! What are you doing?" Sabrina exclaimed.

"Nothing." Salem tried to look innocent. It was hard when he was wearing a red, jeweled turban and purple cape with stars all over it. At least the phone had stopped ringing.

Sabrina folded her arms. "I can always tell when you're lying, Salem."

Salem gulped. "Really? How?"

"Your nose turns green."

"What?" Salem ran to the mirror on the closet door to check. "It is not!"

"Gotcha!" Sabrina said with a grin.

Salem seethed. "What are you doing home, anyway? I thought you went to school."

"I did." She walked to her desk and picked up a book. "But I forgot my math book. So, I just popped home between classes to get it."

"How convenient," Salem griped.

Oh, well. The cat's out of the bag, so to speak. I might as well tell her everything. "All right, I admit it. I'm running a little business out of your room."

"You're what?" Sabrina exclaimed.

"It's for a good cause," Salem said. "So I can pay back Zelda and Hilda."

Sabrina sat down on the bed and picked up his tiny little turban. "So, what kind of business? Costume shop for teeny tiny people?"

Salem lowered his chin and mumbled.

"What was that?"

"Psychic hotline," he whispered.

"Psychic hotline!" she exclaimed. "You're kidding!"

"No, and I'm darn good at it, too," Salem snapped.

Sabrina shook her head. "I can't believe people pay to take advice from a cat."

"They don't know I'm a cat, that's the beauty of it," Salem replied. "Sabrina, please don't tell your aunts. Just a few more days, and I'll be able to pay them back."

"Well . . . I guess I have to admire you for working hard," Sabrina admitted. "And for wanting to do it so you can pay back Aunt Zelda and Aunt Hilda—"

"Oh, thank you, Sabrina," Salem cried.

"*But*—I don't like keeping secrets from them," Sabrina added.

"Don't think of it as a secret," Salem said. "Think of it as a—a surprise."

"Hmmm. I don't know, Salem."

"Just give me one more day," he begged.

"Well . . ."

"How about one more call?" Salem begged. "Please?"

"Okay," Sabrina said. "One more call. But then, you're out of business. Deal?"

Salem stuck out his paw. "Deal."

With a snap of her fingers, Sabrina and her math book disappeared.

Just one more call? Salem griped. *I'll have to keep the person on the line till Halloween!*

He slipped his turban back on and tried to concentrate. "Ring, phone. Ring!"

The phone rang, and Salem pounced on it like a starving cat on a mouse.

"Hello!" he said. "Salem's Psychic Hotline! If you pay me lots of cash, I'll . . . stay on the phone all day with you!" It didn't rhyme, but who cared? He was desperate. "How may I help you?"

Croak, croak.

Salem groaned. *Oh, great. One last shot, and it's that nutty mystery caller with the postnasal drip!*

Oh, well. Salem was a professional. He would just have to work with what fate sent him.

"Speak up!" Salem said encouragingly. "I can't help you if I can't hear you!"

"I-I—I'm shy," the caller croaked.

"Aha! Well, don't worry. Everything here is completely secret. I won't tell anybody if you don't!" Salem chuckled. "What's your name?"

"Uh, Dudley . . ."

"Well, Dud"—Salem had to force himself not to laugh—"tell the Great Salem what your problem is."

"Well," Dudley nearly whispered in a deep hoarse voice, "I—I'm in love."

"Whoa! Have *you* come to the right place!"

"Uh, I don't know," Dudley rasped. "Have I?"

Not again! "Just tell me what's wrong!" Salem snapped.

"This girl . . ." Dudley sighed. It sounded like an old tire going flat. "She's a real sweetheart—a real princess. The most beautiful girl in the world."

Salem had heard it all before. "Sure, sure. So grab her—before someone else does."

"I—I don't know how," Dudley said, then confessed, "I've never even spoken to her."

What a loser! Salem thought. "Why not?"

"Well, I'm not the most handsome guy in the world," he replied. "I'm afraid she won't talk to me. Tell me, Salem," Dudley croaked. "What do you see in my future?

Should I speak to her? Can I ever hope to win her heart?"

Salem closed his eyes. "Psychic Salem hears your question. I pause now to gaze into the future. . . . *Ummm . . . oooh . . . meowwwl . . .*" This was his last call. He had better drag it out as long as possible.

Unlike some of his other customers, this guy waited patiently.

What a sucker, Salem thought. *Lucky for me.*

"*Mmmmmm, ohhhh,*" he groaned, his eyes still closed. "I'm beginning to see the future. I see . . . I see . . ."

Strange. He heard two little sounds. Kind of like soap bubbles popping. Pop, pop!

"I see . . ." He opened his eyes to see what it was. *"Yikes!"*

Hilda and Zelda had just popped into the middle of Sabrina's bedroom. They stared at him with their arms crossed.

"What! What's wrong? What do you see?" the caller gasped.

"Uh, can I call you back?" Salem asked.

The caller gave Salem his number. Then Salem hung up the phone.

Salem smiled at Zelda and Hilda. "An old army buddy," he fibbed.

Zelda snatched the tiny jeweled turban off his head. "Do you always dress like a bad Halloween joke when you talk to old army buddies?"

Salem knew when he was beaten. So he confessed everything. He tried to sound pitiful. Maybe if they felt sorry for him, they wouldn't make him scrub the toilets.

"I was only trying to pay you back," Salem insisted.

But Zelda wasn't buying it. "Sorry, my friend. Salem's Psychic Hotline is officially off the hook. No more calls."

"Just this one?" Salem begged. "Please? I promised I'd call him back!"

"Sorry, Salem," Zelda said. "But you won't be calling anyone back."

"Wh-why?" Salem gasped. "What do you mean?"

Zelda pointed at the phone and said:

"Alex Bell's telephone is one of life's wondrous tools,
But Salem uses it to rip off fools.
So now whenever he speaks into the phone,
The only thing he'll hear is the dial tone."

Zelda pointed at the telephone. It shimmered like gold for a moment. Then looked normal again.

Salem couldn't believe it.

The telephone was his golden goose. His pot of gold. The money-making machine that could rebuild his fortune.

And now—he was locked out for good!

Chapter 7

Boo-hoo-hoo . . ." Salem was crying into the dirty dishes with a tiny white apron tied around him when Sabrina came home from school that afternoon.

"Oh, Salem," Sabrina said. "You look so terrible!"

"You should see my dishpan hands," he wailed.

"What happened?" Sabrina asked.

"Those two mean old witches who pretend to be your sweet little aunties found out about my psychic hotline," Salem told her. "They put me out of business—and back to work!"

Sabrina zapped up an afternoon snack of cookies and milk and sat down at the kitchen table. "Well, it's your own fault you're in trouble," she told him.

"What's a cat supposed to do?" Salem wailed. "There aren't that many ways for a four-legged animal to make money. And I absolutely refuse to do stupid pet tricks. Or join the circus."

Sabrina shrugged. "Wish I could help you."

"That's it!" he cried.

"What's it?" Sabrina asked. "And why do I get the feeling I'm sorry I asked?"

"You can be my assistant," Salem said. "You can make the calls for me. I can hand out the fake answers—I mean, psychic advice. I can still make money, and—"

57

"No way!" Sabrina said.

Salem frowned. "Why not?"

"I told you," Sabrina said. "I think these psychic hotlines are totally fake, and I don't want to be a part of your scam."

"Couldn't you at least help me with that last caller?" Salem asked. "I took his phone number. I promised I'd call him back. You don't want me to break a promise, do you?"

Sabrina hesitated. "Well . . . okay," she said at last. "But just this once. And I'll help you call just so you can tell him that Salem's Psychic Hotline is out of business."

Salem sniffed back a tear and pulled the stopper out of the sink. "Such a beautiful plan . . . down the drain."

Salem dried his paws on a dishtowel, then hopped down.

Sabrina flipped on the speakerphone so

Salem could hear. Then she dialed the last caller's number.

"Hello," the caller croaked. "This is Dudley."

"Um, hi, this is Sabrina. I'm Salem's assistant. From Salem's Psychic Hotline."

"I want to talk to Salem," Dudley said.

"Sorry, he can't come to the phone right now. He's . . . in a trance."

"Oh." The caller cleared his throat. It sounded awful. "Can you help me?"

"Yeah," Sabrina said. "Here's my advice. Take some cold medicine. You sound terrible!"

"I don't have a cold," Dudley said. "This is my normal voice."

"Oh. Uh, sorry," Sabrina said. "But listen, Dudley. I'm calling to tell you that Salem's Psychic Hotline is out of business."

"No!" he said. "You can't do that!"

"We can and we have," Sabrina said, then added kindly. "The Yellow Pages is full of ads for psychic hotlines. Why don't you try one of those? Or better yet, why don't you tell your troubles to a good friend?"

"No," Dudley said. "I don't know what it is. But I feel a very special connection to Salem. A psychic connection. As if he and I had something very deep in common. Only Salem will do. Please?" he croaked. "I'm desperate. I'm rich. Very rich. Tell him I'll offer him gold if he'll help me."

"Gold?" Salem gasped from his perch on the couch. "Did he say gold?" Without thinking, Salem grabbed at the phone.

ZZZZZZZTTTTT!

"Yowl!" Salem stuck his zapped paw in his mouth. He had forgotten about Zelda's spell.

He quickly yelled into the phone: "I'll meet you in person!"

"Where?" the caller asked.

"At the bench by the pond in the park!"
Hummmmmm.

Salem's voice had activated the spell's hang-up feature.

But Salem wasn't upset. He was too busy thinking about the gold. This was the answer to all his problems!

"I don't think so," Sabrina drawled, folding her arms. "There's no way you can show up for a meeting with this caller."

"And why not?" Salem demanded.

"Because," Sabrina reminded him. "You're a cat. Remember? A *talking* cat. And who in his right mind would give gold to a cat?"

Oh, no! Salem thought. He couldn't miss out on this. It was the opportunity of a lifetime! What could he do?

I've got to find a way!

Chapter 8

$\mathbb{S}$alem paced the back of the couch, his tail swishing like a question mark.

"I've got it!" he cried at last. He looked up at Sabrina. He put on his best adorable-cat face.

"You can come along and pretend to be my assistant," Salem told Sabrina. "I'll just whisper my advice in your ear. You can give the caller his advice. And pick up my reward for me."

"Okay," Sabrina said reluctantly. "But only because I feel sorry for the guy who called!"

It was dusk when they reached Westbridge City Park. The streetlights were just coming on.

They could hear the crickets playing their night music. They could hear the croak of frogs in the nearby pond.

Sabrina sat down on a park bench. Salem hopped up beside her.

"It's getting dark," Sabrina said. "I don't see anybody. Maybe he's not coming."

"Just be patient, Sabrina," Salem whispered in her ear. "Good things come to those who wait. And gold is definitely a good thing."

Suddenly they heard a voice. A deep croaky voice. "Hi."

Sabrina jumped to her feet. She peered

63

into the shadows, but she couldn't see anybody. "Who's there?"

"It's me, Dudley."

"This is too spooky," Sabrina said. "I can't talk to you if I can't see you."

"Why not? That never stopped Salem on the phone before," Dudley said.

"This is different,"

"How?"

"Because *you* can see *us.*"

"Us?"

"Uh, me and my cat."

Dudley sighed. It sounded like a whoopee cushion. "Okay. But I warned you. I'm pretty ugly."

"Looks aren't important," Sabrina said.

Salem looked around. How ugly could he be? But nobody stepped forward from the shadows.

"Okay, here I am."

Sabrina and Salem looked around. They didn't see anybody.

"Where?" Sabrina asked.

"Down here!"

Sabrina and Salem followed the sound.

Sitting at Sabrina's feet, staring up at them, was a frog. A bumpy, bug-eyed, slimy frog.

"So," the frog said. "I'm Dudley. Now you know my problem. How are you going to help me?"

Chapter 9

$\mathcal{S}$alem couldn't hold his tongue. "*You're* the mysterious caller?" he blurted out.

"Croak!" Dudley the frog blurted in amazement. "*You're* a talking cat?"

"So this is amazing to a talking frog?" Sabrina said.

"I'm Salem," Salem said.

"A psychic kitty?" the frog said in amazement. "No *wonder* I felt such a connection to you. We have a lot in common. What's your story?"

Salem sighed. "I was a normal warlock. Till I got caught trying to take over the world. The Witches' Council turned me into a cat for a hundred years. It's pretty tough."

"Tell me about it," Dudley croaked.

"So what happened to you?" Salem asked.

"Well, it's a long story," Dudley said. "I had a little run-in with a real witch a while back." He glanced at Sabrina. "Uh, not a nice one like you. A real wicked witch. And the rest is history."

"Were you a handsome prince?" Sabrina asked.

"Oh, you heard?" the frog said.

"Uh, I read about it," Sabrina said.

Salem frowned. "Wouldn't it fix everything if you just got this girl to kiss you? Wouldn't you just turn back into a handsome prince?"

Dudley shrugged sadly. "That only happens in fairy tales. Besides, I'm too shy even to talk to her. Much less get her to kiss me. That's what I wanted to know from you, Salem. Do you see a romance for me with this girl in the future? Or should I just give it up?"

"Hmm," Salem said. "Let me consult with my assistant."

He led Sabrina a few yards away from the frog so they could talk.

"There's only one way any princess is going to fall in love with Dudley," Salem whispered.

"How?" Sabrina wondered.

Salem rolled his eyes. "You have to turn him back into a handsome prince!"

Sabrina shook her head. "Don't you remember what my aunts and my dad always say? *Terrrrrrrrible* things can happen when a witch messes around in the lives of mortals."

"But this guy isn't a mortal," Salem reminded her. "He's a frog. Plus, he's got gold."

"Okay, okay," Sabrina said. "I'll try. It's not so easy to break another witch's spell, you know. Especially when you don't know the witch. We all have our own style—"

"Please try," Salem said.

"All right. But I don't know if it will work." Sabrina went over to the little ugly frog. She pushed her sleeves up and thought. "Okay, here goes:

>*"Frog so ugly it makes me wince,*
>*Turn back into a handsome prince."*

She zapped the frog with a bolt of lightning from her fingertip.

A strange, smoky swamp smell struck their nostrils.

Salem and Sabrina peered into the sparkly purple green smoke.

Did it work?

Chapter 10

 t last the smoke cleared.

Salem coughed, then looked.

"It worked!" he cried.

The frog looked like a handsome prince. A prince right out of a storybook. Or right out of *Teen People* magazine.

"Whoa! Do I do cute, or what?" Sabrina whispered to Salem.

"Give it up, Sabrina," Salem whispered back. "He's got his heart set on another."

"That's okay," Sabrina replied. "Harvey's a prince to me." She smiled at Dudley. "That wicked witch must have been pretty mad."

"I guess so," Dudley said. "She was in a pretty big hurry that day—something about selling apples to a girl named Snow White."

Dudley looked down at his arms and legs. He ran to the pond and studied his reflection in the water. "I can't believe it!"

He plucked a wildflower from the bank. "Wow! How wonderful to have fingers again!"

Then he bowed like a prince and presented the flower to Sabrina. "Thanks, my lady, for everything." Then he kissed her hand.

Sabrina blushed. "Oh, hey, no problem."

"You'll get my bill in the mail," Salem purred. "Now, get out of here. Go find that princess and live happily ever after."

"Really?" the prince asked hopefully. "You think she'll want me now?"

Salem nodded. "Salem has spoken."

The frog prince hopped off happily to find his girl.

"Well, that worked out pretty well, I guess," Sabrina had to admit.

"Yes," Salem drawled. "If all goes well, I'll soon have a bag full of gold."

Sabrina was home when the phone rang the next day.

She hoped it was Harvey. If he finished with his Saturday chores, they were going skating in the park.

"Hello? Harvey?" she asked hopefully.

"NO! This is not Harvey!" the caller said.

Sabrina covered the mouthpiece of the phone with her hand. "Salem! It's Dudley the frog prince. And it sounds like he's hopping mad!"

"What!" Salem leaped onto the couch beside Sabrina. "He should be married and on his honeymoon by now. Turn on the speakerphone so I can hear."

Sabrina pressed the button.

". . . and I've got a message for that con artist, Salem Saberhagen!"

Salem's golden eyes widened. The hair on his back stood up. He started to speak.

Sabrina held up her hand. "Shhh. Remember? Your voice will activate the shut-off feature of Aunt Zelda's spell."

"Oh, yeah," Salem whispered. "Well, then, go ahead. Ask him what happened!"

"So, Prince Dudley," Sabrina said. "Calm down. Tell us what happened."

"I went to see the object of my affections and ask her out. I thought I was looking pretty cool."

"Well? Did you ask her out?" Sabrina asked.

"No!" the frog prince croaked.

"Why not?" Sabrina demanded.

73

"She wouldn't even look at me!" he complained.

"No!"

"Yes," Dudley said mournfully. "In fact, she was so turned off by the way I looked that she ran away!"

"What?" Salem and Sabrina looked at each other in surprise.

"I can't believe it!" Salem whispered.

"I can't, either," Sabrina whispered back. "I made him so cute. If I weren't so crazy about Harvey, I might even ask him out myself. It doesn't make any sense."

Salem paced along the back of the couch, thinking. "Tell him we'll meet him in the park. Same place. We *have* to work this out."

"But what if there's nothing you can do, O Great One?" Sabrina asked.

"We have to figure it out," Salem said. He leaped to the floor and ran to the front door. "There's too much gold at stake!"

Chapter 11

Sabrina snapped her fingers. *Whoosh!* Seconds later she and Salem stood in the park.

The frog prince sat at the same park bench. He sat on the ground with his head in his hands.

"He looks pretty depressed," Sabrina whispered.

"Hello, Dudley," Salem called out.

The prince sprang to his feet. "There you are, you mangy cat! I ought to turn you over to the animal shelter! I ought to tell them to lock you up and throw away the key! I ought to—"

"Wait a minute, hold on," Sabrina interrupted.

"There must be some kind of . . . interference, yes, that's it, interference here," Salem told Dudley. "But don't worry. I've got an idea."

"What?" the prince asked. "I'll try anything."

"Take us to where this girl of yours lives," Salem suggested. "Maybe that will help us figure it out."

The prince gave Sabrina directions. She snapped her fingers and—*whoosh!*—they were there.

"Whoa, this girl must be loaded!" Salem exclaimed.

Her home was a castle—a mansion really. It sat on a hill surrounded by beautiful gardens.

"I told you she was a real princess," the frog prince said.

"I thought that was a figure of speech," Salem gasped. "I didn't know you meant a *real* one."

They sneaked into the beautiful gardens. Lush ferns and flowers grew around a charming pond covered with lily pads.

Salem headed toward the tree-lined walkway that led to the castle.

"Not that way!" the frog prince whispered. "She's not up there."

"No?" Salem looked around. "Where is she then?"

"She's here," Dudley said. "In the garden."

Salem walked around, his tail swishing. "Where?" he said.

He looked in the gazebo.

No princess.

He looked in the rowboat.

No princess.

"Over there," the prince croaked.

Salem looked around. The prince was pointing at the pond.

"Oh, my goodness—she's drowned herself?" Salem cried. "Quick, Sabrina! Try to save her!"

"No, no, no," the prince said impatiently. "There!"

He pointed at the pond again. At a lily pad in the middle of the pond.

Salem squinted. *No, it can't be!*

"Oh, my!" Sabrina exclaimed. "Your 'beautiful princess' is—"

"A bumpy, warty, bug-eyed, slimy frog!" Salem gasped.

"Isn't she beautiful?" the prince sighed.

"What a cute little crown," Sabrina cooed.

"Never mind that!" Salem snapped. "Why didn't you tell us she was a frog!" he asked the prince. "No wonder your human form frightened her away!

"Sabrina," Salem whispered. "Do something! Turn her into a beautiful princess or something! Or I'll never get paid!"

Sabrina pushed up her sleeves. She cast a magic spell, a spell fit for a fairy tale:

"Human, animal, witch, or elf,
To find true love, just be yourself!"

A puff of greenish smoke filled the air. When the smoke cleared, Salem looked hopefully toward the pond.

"It didn't work!" he moaned.

"Sure it did," Sabrina said.

"But the frog princess is still a frog," Salem wailed.

Sabrina smiled and shook her head. "Salem, you're looking at it all wrong. Take a closer look." She pointed down at their feet.

That's when Salem realized what had really happened. The magic spell hadn't turned the girl frog into a beautiful prin-

79

cess. It had turned the handsome prince back into a frog!

But Dudley was still shy. So Sabrina wiggled her finger and flew him right onto the lily pad next to the frog princess.

"Croak," he managed to say. "H-hello, Wanda."

The frog princess gasped in surprise. Her eyes opened wide. She seemed frozen in shock.

"Oh, no," Salem muttered. "Don't run away again!"

The frog princess didn't run. She leaped.

But not away.

As soon as she laid eyes on the ugly little frog, she flipped—and flung herself into his arms.

Dudley the happy frog prince winked at Sabrina. He tossed Salem a cloth bag. Then he hopped into the pond with his bride.

Sabrina sighed. "And they lived happily

every after." She turned to Salem and whispered, "I guess it's just like that old saying, 'Beauty is in the eye of the beholder.'"

"Yeah," Salem whispered gleefully as he pawed open the sack. "Woo-hoo! And gold is in the hands of the Psychic Kitty!"

Chapter 12

A week later things were back to normal in the Spellman house. Or at least as normal as they could be in a house where three witches and a talking cat lived.

Now when the phone rang, it was usually Sabrina's friends Harvey or Val.

One night Sabrina and her aunts were watching a *Bewitched* marathon on TV. Salem dozed on the back of the couch.

Just then a commercial for the Psychic Pals Hotline came on.

Sabrina quickly snatched up the remote

control and changed the channel to an all-news channel until the commercial was over.

"So," Aunt Zelda said, "did you learn your lesson, Salem?"

"You bet," Salem replied. He had paid Zelda back for the phone bill. She and Hilda had made him give a part of his money to the Homeless Frogs Society. He even had a little left over to put into stocks. "It's definitely too risky to give people advice. But I'm glad I was able to help Dudley and Wanda. I hope they live happily ever—"

Salem broke off when he heard the news reporter say, "Stocks took a big dive today when . . ."

But Sabrina was already clicking back to *Bewitched*.

They watched for a while, then Sabrina noticed that their chatty black cat had stopped commenting on everything that happened in the show. "Hey, where's Salem?"

Her aunts exchanged a worried glance. They didn't have to be psychics to think that the sudden disappearance of Salem the talking cat meant trouble.

Sabrina and her aunts tiptoed upstairs to Sabrina's room. They slowly opened the door and peeked inside.

Salem sat on Sabrina's bed with his little paws on a Ouija Board. It was a game board one could buy in any store. But some people thought it could tell their fortune or predict the future.

"Tell me about the stock market," Salem asked the Ouija Board. "Should I buy or sell?"

"Salem!" Sabrina cried. "What are you doing?"

Salem jumped and the Ouija Board crashed to the floor.

"Hey," he said with a shrug. "You can't blame a cat for trying!"

Cat Care Tips

#1 Some cats love to be brushed, others hate it. You do not need to brush your cat unless it is a long-hair cat whose fur becomes matted.

#2 Healthy cats do not need baths. They clean themselves very well. Baths are very stressful to cats and should be avoided unless otherwise instructed by your veterinarian.

#3 Cats should be handled gently—do not squeeze them too tightly when you hug them. Never pull on their tails.

—Laura E. Smiley, MS, DVM, Dipl. ACVIM
Gwynedd Veterinary Hospital